DISCOVER!

ANIMALS THAT SLITHER AND SLIDE

SLIMY SNAILS

BY THERESA EMMINIZER

Please visit our website, www.enslow.com. For a free color catalog of all our high-quality books, call toll free 1-800-398-2504 or fax 1-877-980-4454.

Library of Congress Cataloging-in-Publication Data
Names: Emminizer, Theresa, author.
Title: Slimy snails / Theresa Emminizer.
Description: Buffalo : Enslow Publishing, [2024] | Series: Animals that slither and slide | Includes index.
Identifiers: LCCN 2023029813 (print) | LCCN 2023029814 (ebook) | ISBN 9781978537354 (library binding) | ISBN 9781978537347 (paperback) | ISBN 9781978537361 (ebook)
Subjects: LCSH: Snails–Juvenile literature.
Classification: LCC QL430.4 .E67 2024 (print) | LCC QL430.4 (ebook) | DDC 594/.3–dc23/eng/20230713
LC record available at https://lccn.loc.gov/2023029813
LC ebook record available at https://lccn.loc.gov/2023029814

First Edition

Published in 2024 by
Enslow Publishing
2544 Clinton Street
Buffalo, NY 14224

Designer: Leslie Taylor
Editor: Theresa Emminizer

Photo credits: Cover (snail) Marko Blagoevic/Shutterstock.com, (slime background) AMarc/Shutterstock.com, (brush stroke) Sonic_S/Shutterstock.com, (slime frame) klyaksun/Shutterstock.com; Series Art (slime blob) Lemberg Vector studio/Shutterstock.com; p. 5 Andrei Armiagov/Shutterstock.com; p. 7 Peter Cripps/Shutterstock.com; p. 9 sweet marshmallow/Shutterstock.com; p. 11 Krittiya Siriwal/Shutterstock.com; p. 13 Mark Brandon/Shutterstock.com; p. 15 Chalosimo/Shutterstock.com; p. 17 LTim/Shutterstock.com; p. 19 Sergey Lavrentev/Shutterstock.com; p. 21 Andrzej Rostek/Shutterstock.com.

Printed in the United States of America

CPSIA compliance information: Batch #CW24ENS: For further information contact Enslow Publishing, at 1-800-398-2504.

CONTENTS

Boldface words appear in Words to Know.

SNAILS, SNAILS EVERYWHERE!

Have you ever seen a slimy little snail in your garden? Snails are cute little shelled animals that can be found almost everywhere. Some live on land and some in water. In this book, we'll talk about land snails.

Snails are a kind of animal called gastropods.

ALL SORTS OF SNAILS

The African giant snail is the biggest land snail. The largest of the **species** was 15.5 inches (39.3 cm) long and weighed 2 pounds (907 g)! The smallest land snail is only about the size of a piece of sand!

The shell of the largest African giant snail was 10.75 inches (27.3 cm).

A SNAIL'S BODY

Snails' bodies have four main parts: the visceral hump, mantle, head, and foot. The visceral hump is underneath the shell. It holds most of the snail's **organs**. The mantle is the shell's fleshy lining. Snails move along on their **muscly** foot.

VISCERAL HUMP
(UNDER SHELL)
SHELL
HEAD
MANTLE
FOOT

Snails have small parts called tentacles on top of their head. The eyes are on top of the tentacles. The snail's mouth is at the base of its head. The mouth is filled with two rows of tiny teeth.

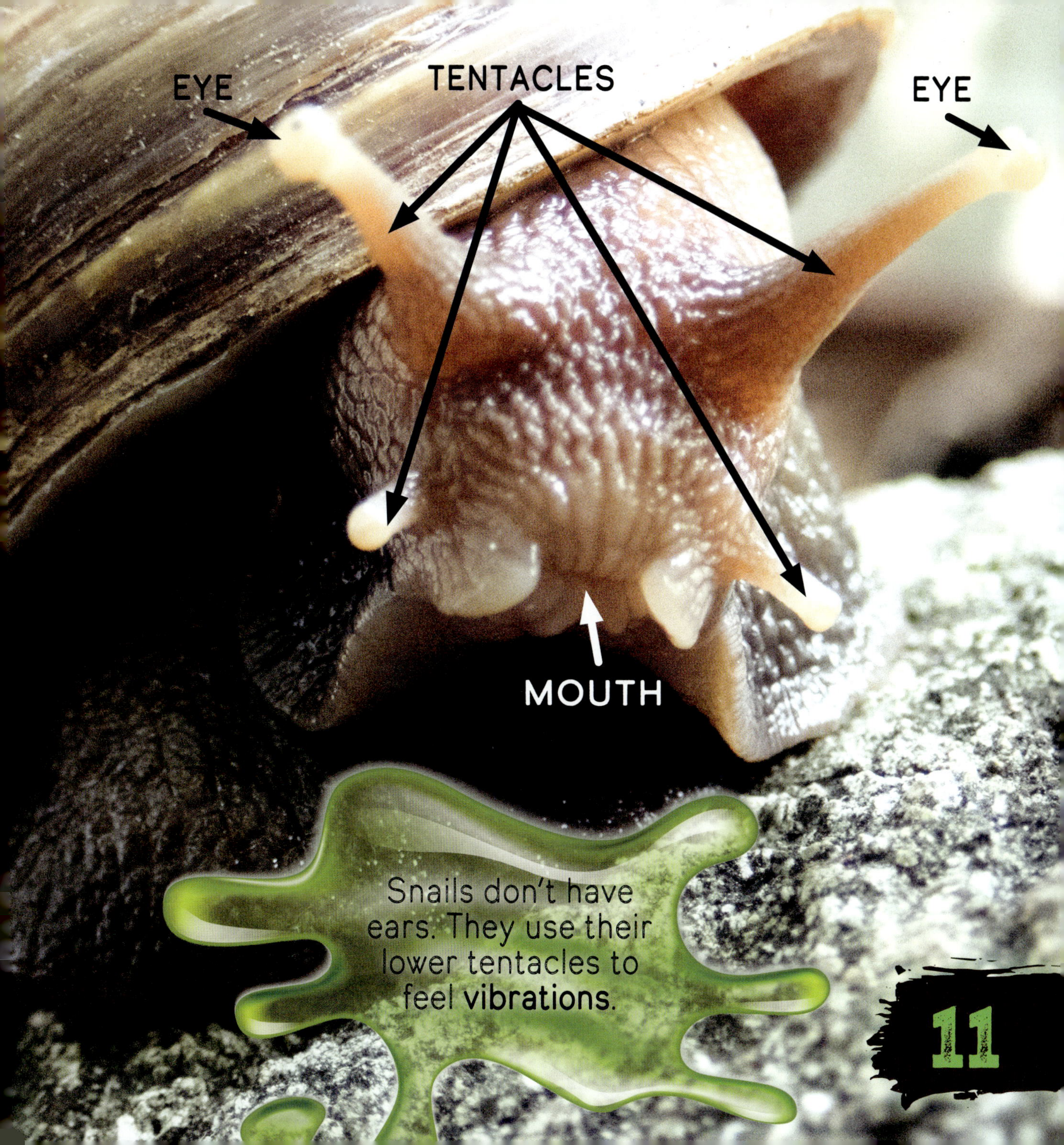

Snails don't have ears. They use their lower tentacles to feel **vibrations**.

SNAIL SHELLS

Snails are invertebrates, meaning they don't have backbones. But they do have shells to keep them safe. Snails don't change their shell as they grow. Instead, the shell grows with them. You can guess a snail's age based on the number of swirls on its shell.

Usually snails can pull their head and foot into their shell.

SNAIL TRAIL

Have you ever seen the slimy trail left behind by a snail? That's mucus! Mucus is a kind of jelly that snails make. Mucus helps snails slide along rough, or bumpy, **surfaces**. It also helps them stick to things!

Snails can crawl up walls or even upside down!

Snails also make mucus to keep themselves wet when it's too dry outside. New mucus is always being made. This keeps **germs** off the snail's body. Some snails also use mucus to keep themselves safe from predators!

Some people put snail mucus on their skin to keep it soft!

A SNAIL'S PACE

Snails are known for moving slowly. But they aren't as slow as people think! Snails move about 3.3 feet (1 m) per hour. The world's fastest land snail moved at 0.06 mile (0.1 km) per hour.

Snails
can't move
backward!

LIFE OF A SNAIL

Most snails are hermaphrodites, meaning they have both male and female parts. Just one garden snail can have up to 430 babies in a year! Different species live for different lengths of time, but most garden snails live one to three years.

Snail babies **hatch** from eggs.

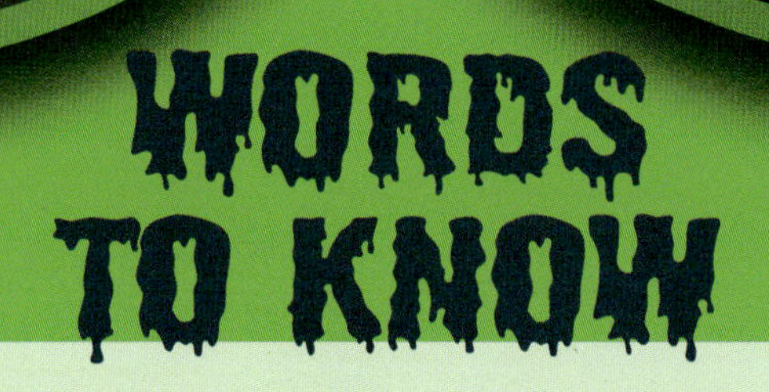

germ: A tiny organism that can cause disease.

hatch: To break out of an egg.

muscly: Strong or made of muscle, or one of the parts of the body that allow movement.

organ: A part inside an animal's body.

species: A group of plants or animals that are all of the same kind.

surface: The top layer of something.

vibration: A rapid movement back and forth.

FOR MORE INFORMATION

BOOKS

Podmorow, Ava. *Snails.* Oliver, BC, Canada: Engage Books, 2022.

Markovics, Joyce L. *Yellow-Tipped Oahu Tree Snail.* Ann Arbor, MI: Cherry Lake Publishing, 2023.

WEBSITES

Bio Kids
www.biokids.umich.edu/critters/Achatina_fulica/
Learn more about the African giant snail.

Why Do Snails Leave Slime Trails?
www.wonderopolis.org/wonder/why-do-snails-leave-slime-trails
Find out more about a snail's special mucus here!

Publisher's note to educators and parents: Our editors have carefully reviewed these websites to ensure that they are suitable for students. Many websites change frequently, however, and we cannot guarantee that a site's future contents will continue to meet our high standards of quality and educational value. Be advised that students should be closely supervised whenever they access the internet.

INDEX